**Dear Parents,**

Welcome to the Scholastic Reader series. We [illegible] years of experience with teachers, parents, a[illegible] into a program that is designed to match your child's interests and skills.

**Level 1**—Short sentences and stories made up of words kids can sound out using their phonics skills and words that are important to remember.

**Level 2**—Longer sentences and stories with words kids need to know and new "big" words that they will want to know.

**Level 3**—From sentences to paragraphs to longer stories, these books have large "chunks" of texts and are made up of a rich vocabulary.

**Level 4**—First chapter books with more words and fewer pictures.

It is important that children learn to read well enough to succeed in school and beyond. Here are ideas for reading this book with your child:

- Look at the book together. Encourage your child to read the title and make a prediction about the story.
- Read the book together. Encourage your child to sound out words when appropriate. When your child struggles, you can help by providing the word.
- Encourage your child to retell the story. This is a great way to check for comprehension.
- Have your child take the fluency test on the last page to check progress.

Scholastic Readers are designed to support your child's efforts to learn how to read at every age and every stage. Enjoy helping your child learn to read and love to read.

**—Francie Alexander**
Chief Education Officer
Scholastic Education

Copyright © 1995 by Nancy Hall, Inc.
Fluency activities copyright © 2003 Scholastic Inc.

All rights reserved. Published by Scholastic Inc.
SCHOLASTIC, CARTWHEEL BOOKS, and associated logos are trademarks
and/or registered trademarks of Scholastic Inc.

Library of Congress Cataloging-in-Publication Data is available.

ISBN 0-439-59415-4

10 9 8 7                                                          09  10  11  12  13/0

Printed in the U.S.A.     23
First printing, January 1995

# by Paul Fehlner
# Illustrated by Laura Rader

**Scholastic Reader — Level 1**

Cartwheel
·B·O·O·K·S·®

SCHOLASTIC INC.

New York   Toronto   London   Auckland   Sydney
Mexico City   New Delhi   Hong Kong   Buenos Aires

"It's time to get up," said Mommy.

"No way," I said.

"Get up," said Mommy.

I got up.

"Eggs for breakfast," said Daddy.

"No way," I said.

"Breakfast," said Daddy.

# I ate eggs for breakfast.

"I want to go play," I said.
"No way," said Mommy.

"I want to see Grandma,"
said Daddy.

I did not go play.

"I want to sit up front," I said.
"No way," said Daddy.

"No way," said Mommy.

I did not sit up front.

"I want cookies," I said.
"Okay?" said Grandma.

# Mommy and Daddy said okay.

# I love Grandma.

# Let's Talk...

The child in this story must do what her parents want her to do.

What are some of the things her parents want her to do?

How do you think she feels? Why?

# Time for O

All of these words have the letter **O** in them:

for    to    love    no

Mommy        cookies

front   go   okay   not

Point to the letter **O** in each of the words.

Can you find a word that starts with **O**?

Can you find three words that end with **O**?

Can you find a word that has two **O**'s in it?

# Order These!

The pictures in each row tell a story. But they are all mixed up! What happens first? Next? Next? What happens last?

# Some Days

Did you ever have a day when it seemed as if you never got to do what you wanted to do? Tell about it. What did you really want to do? What did you do instead?

# Opposites Time

Words that are opposites mean something complete-ly different. Hot and cold are opposites. Big and little are opposites, too.

For each word on the left, point to the word on the right side that means the opposite.

no                    down

go                    back

front                 stop

up                    yes

# Which One Doesn't Belong?

In each row, one item does not belong with the others.
Point to the item that does not belong.

# Answers

(*Let's Talk*)  Answers will vary.

(*Time for O*)

    starts with **O**: okay

    ends with **O**: to, go, no

    has 2 **O**'s: cookies

(*Some Days*)  Answers will vary.

(*Order These*)

(*Opposites Time*)

no        down
go        back
front      stop
up        yes

(*Which One Doesn't Belong?*)